RUTH E. SALTZMAN

POPPY BEAR

THE GARDEN THAT OVERSLEPT

ILLUSTRATED BY CATHERINE DEETER

BEYOND
WORDS
Publishing
I N C

Beyond Words Publishing, Inc.

20827 N.W. Cornell Road, Suite 500

Hillsboro, Oregon 97124-9808

503-531-8700/1-800-284-9673

www.beyondword.com

Editor: Michelle Roehm

Design: Principia Graphica

Illustrations: Catherine Deeter

Printed in Hong Kong

Distributed to the book trade by Publishers Group West

Library of Congress Cataloging-in-Publication Data

Saltzman, Ruth E.

    Poppy Bear : the garden that overslept / by Ruth E. Saltzman ; illustrated by Catherine Deeter.

       p. cm.

    Summary: Two curious children, wondering why Spring is late, find Poppy Bear in their garden and he teaches them about the beauty of nature and their role in caring for it as they plant seeds and flowers together.

    ISBN 1-58270-042-7

       [1. Spring--Fiction. 2. Bears--Fiction. 3. Gardening--Fiction. 3. Ecology--Fiction. 5. Stories in rhyme.] I. Deeter, Catherine, ill. II. Title.

    PZ8.3.S178 Po 2000

    [E]--dc21   00-045438

The corporate mission of Beyond Words Publishing, Inc.:

Inspire to Integrity

To
Ida & David

For my children, grandchildren, and always Prince Hal.
—*R.E.S.*

For my grandmother Claudine, gardener and artist.
—*C.D.*

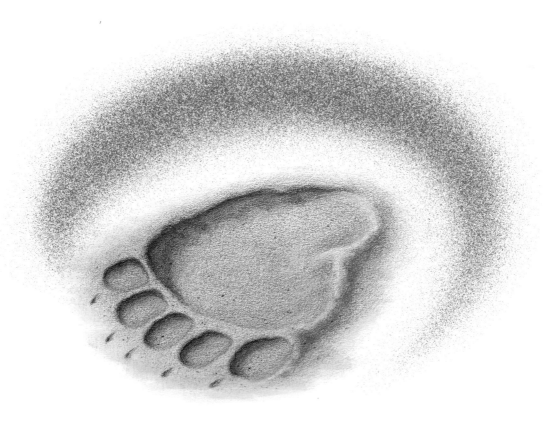

PROLOGUE

Once upon a moon ago, springtime was missing...

Looking out of her kitchen window, David and Ida's mother sighed. "It is time for spring, but it still seems like winter. It's so cold and there are no flowers!" Shaking her head, she added, "It just isn't springtime without flowers." Then she turned to her children and whispered, somewhat mysteriously, "Springtime is...missing!"

"Missing?" asked Ida. "What happened?"

"Don't worry, Mom," said David. "We'll find out. We'll find some flowers for you."

"That would be very nice," their mother replied, turning back to the window and smiling to herself.

...So David and Ida ran out in search of spring...

he time for spring had come and gone,
but everything seemed wrong.
There were no leaves upon the trees.
There were no birds... no song.

The garden was a lifeless place
with everything so bare.
They searched for sprouts; they searched for buds;
but there was nothing there.

Around and 'round the garden
they hunted for a flower.
The children looked in every nook;
it took more than an hour.

Oh, they looked high and they looked low;
no flowers could be found.
Just then—they heard a blust'ry snore
from *Something* on the ground!

Brave David called out, "Who is there?"
Just silence… not a sound.
Was that a **howl?**… Was that a **growl?**
That *Something's* large — and round!

A sleeping bear was snoring there,
but there's no need to worry.
His paws were gold; his nose was cold,
and he was brown and furry.

No need to worry, 'cause this bear
was in a funny pose,
and flowers were popping from his hair
and growing 'round his toes!

Right near his paws, beside his claws,
there was the strangest thing:
a chain of gold, a watch that told
the time as "Half-Past Spring!"

"We're sorry to disturb you, Sir,"
they whispered, "Beg your pardon,
are you aware that you are sleeping
loudly in our garden?"

Awakening, the bear did sigh,
"I'm feeling so inept,
for spring has almost passed us by.
I fear I've overslept!

"Please let me introduce myself.
My name is Poppy Bear.
You're Ida? And you're David?
Why, I'd know you *anywhere!*"

"How do?" they both said to the bear.
"How do?" the bear replied.
"My friends, I've been expecting you.
So glad you have arrived.

"Now that you're here, no time to waste!
I haven't done a thing!
There's seeds to sow and flowers to grow—
it's time to bring back spring!"

Quick as a wink, he raised his paws,
and then they saw the shimmer
of sparkling seeds and petals
floating in a golden glimmer.

He reached into his pocket vest,
and gave them both some seed.
"A bit of this, a shake of that,
is all that you will need.

"Seeds lead to grand adventures
and great discoveries!
Now, plant them where it's sunny,
not shaded by the trees."

He spread his claws and scratched the ground,
then gave *himself* a shake.
"I find it most convenient
to carry my own rake!"

But then he paused and growled perplexed,
"Gr-rr! Human son and daughter,
we have a little problem here.
We're going to need some water!"

A puffy cloud high in the sky
was watching all the fuss.
Poppy Bear looked up and waved,
"Friend, come and rain on us!"

The children danced, and Poppy pranced,
as raindrops splashed their hair.
And flowers grew in Poppy's tracks
while rainbows filled the air.

Then there arose a wondrous throng
of animals and bees,
and butterflies and hummingbirds,
wildflowers, and sweet peas.

Grand tiger lilies, dandelions,
and monkey-flowers, too.
Foxgloves howled! And dogwoods growled!
It was almost like a zoo!

A multitude of songbirds sang
along with frogs and bugs;
and squirrels danced upon the grass
with chipmunks, snails and slugs.

All gathered in a grand parade,
they marched around the trees,
in and out and 'round-about…
while spreading sparkling seeds.

A caterpillar cried to them,
"*I want so much to fly*.
But I've no wings or paws or things—
how can I even try?"

Then Poppy smiled and gently growled,
"Things aren't what they may seem,
for life has *wonderful* things in store.
No dream is impossible—dream!"

The caterpillar smiled at them
and spun a golden case
that gradually enveloped her
without a single trace.

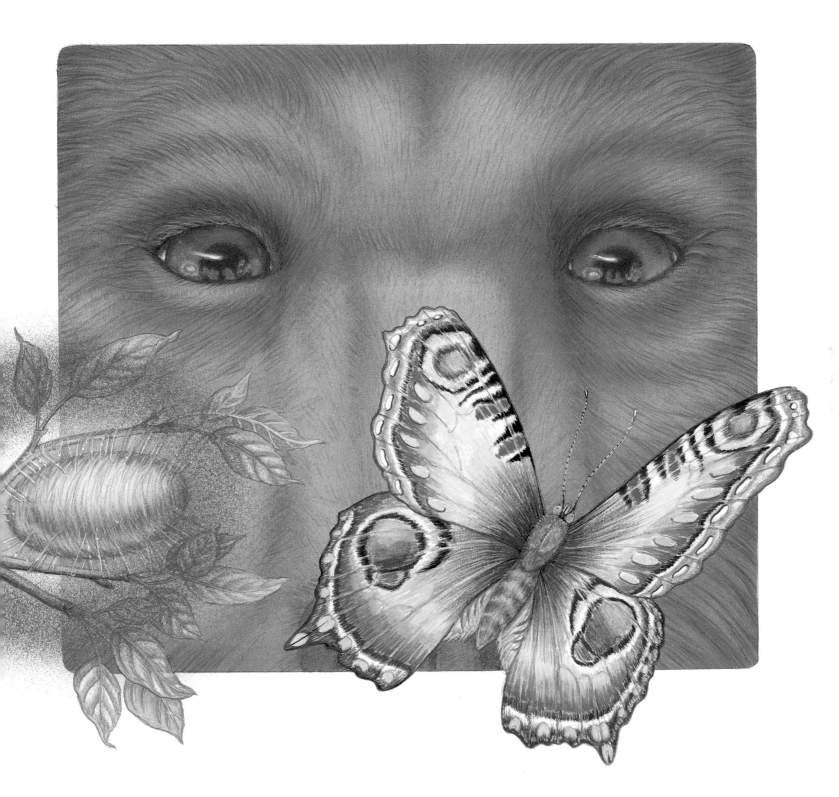

As Poppy touched the small cocoon
with both his golden paws,
a brilliant butterfly emerged
to all of their applause.

The garden had come back to life
that hours before seemed dead.
The children laughed with Poppy Bear.
"Quite magical!" he said.

A spider spun a golden web—
it was the final touch.
Poppy softly said to her,
"Why, thank you very much."

The time had come to say goodbye,
and deep in Poppy's eyes,
the children saw bright meadow flowers
and endless springtime skies.

Then with a bow, he said, "Farewell!
Now don't be sad, my dears.
My love's still here surrounding you.
And I'll be back next year!"

Without a sound, he disappeared,
and there upon the ground
a drift of poppies blossomed in
a golden glowing mound.

Then music swirled around them
and the wind sang Poppy's tune.
They listened till it faded,
and then whispered, "Come back soon!"

They both ran home, arms full of flowers,
with wondrous tales to share
of seeds and talking butterflies
and a giant magic bear!

Their mother smiled at what she heard,
recalling days of old,
when as a child she also met
the Bear with Paws of Gold.

So Ida knew, now you do, too,
why spring was on vacation.
It was because four golden paws
had been in hibernation.

Oh, springtimes come, and springtimes go,
but David always knows—
there *is* a bear, a *dancing* bear,
with flowers 'round his toes.

Dear Children Everywhere,
    Please take care of my garden.
There's still so much to do.
A garden needs a gardener.
Can I depend on you?
All the Earth's a garden.
As you grow, you'll know that's true.
Look for me where flowers bloom.
I'll be seeing you!
            Love,
            Poppy Bear